71

D0492619

Enid Blyton

THE CHRISTMAS STORY

Illustrated by Alan Fraser

RED FOX

EARLY TWO THOUSAND YEARS AGO THERE LIVED IN the town of Nazareth in Palestine a girl called Mary. One day an angel came to her with great news.

'Hail, Mary!' said the angel. 'I bring you great tidings. You will have a little baby boy, and you must call him Jesus. He shall be great, and shall be called the Son of the Highest. He will be the Son of God, and of his kingdom there shall be no end.'

Now Mary was only a little village girl, and she could hardly believe this news; but as she gazed up at the angel, she knew that it was true. She was full of joy and wonder. She was to have a baby boy of her own, and He was to be the little Son of God.

Mary married a carpenter called Joseph, and together they lived in a little house on the hillside. She could hear him hammering at his work, as she went about the little house. Her heart sang as she thought of the tiny baby who was to come to her that winter.

The summer went by, and it was autumn. Then the winter came – and with it arrived men who put up a big notice in the town. Mary went to read it.

It was a notice saying that everyone must go to their own home-town and pay taxes. This meant that Mary and Joseph must leave Nazareth, and go to Bethlehem, for that was where their families came from.

Mary did not feel very strong just then, and the thought of the long walk to Bethlehem filled her with dismay. But Joseph comforted her.

'You shall ride on the donkey,' he said. 'I will walk beside you. We shall be three or four days on the way, but the little donkey will take you easily.'

So Mary and Joseph set off to go to Bethlehem. Mary rode on the little donkey, and Joseph walked beside her, leading it. Many other people were on the roads too, for everyone had to go to pay their taxes. Mary and Joseph travelled for some days, and one night Mary felt tired.

'When shall we be there?' said Mary. 'I feel tired. I want to lie down and rest.'

'There are the lights of Bethlehem,' said Joseph, pointing through the darkness to where some lights twinkled. 'We shall soon be there.'

'Shall we find room at Bethlehem?' said Mary. 'There are so many people going there.'

'We will go to an inn,' said Joseph. 'There you will find warmth and food, comfort and rest. We shall soon be there.'

When they had climbed down the hill to the town of Bethlehem, Mary felt so tired that she longed to go to the inn at once.

'Here it is,' said Joseph, and he stopped the little donkey before a building that was well-lighted, and from which came the sounds of voices and laughter. Then Joseph called for the inn-keeper, and a man came to the door, holding up a lantern so that he might see the travellers.

'Can you give us a room quickly?' said Joseph. 'My wife is very tired, and needs to rest at once.'

'My inn is full, and there is not a bed to be had in the whole town. People have been coming here all day long,' said the inn-keeper. 'You will find nowhere to sleep. There is no room at the inn.'

'Can't you find us a resting-place somewhere?' said Joseph, anxiously. 'My wife has come so far and is so tired.'

The man swung his lantern up to look at Mary, who sat patiently on the donkey, waiting. He saw how tired she was, how white her face looked, and how patiently she sat there. He was filled with pity, and he wondered what he could do.

'I have a cave at the back of my inn, where my oxen sleep,' he said. 'Your wife could lie there. I will have it swept for you, and new straw put down. But that is the best I can offer you.'

'Let me lie in the stable, Joseph,' said Mary. 'I cannot go any farther now.'

So Joseph said they would sleep in the cave that night. Whilst a servant swept out the stall where they were to lie, he helped Mary off the donkey. She walked wearily round to the cave in the hillside, and saw the servant putting down piles of clean straw for her. From nearby stalls big-eyed oxen stared round, munching, wondering who had come to share their stable that night. Doves on the rafters took

their heads from under their wings, and watched with bright eyes.

Mary lay down in the straw. Joseph looked after her tenderly. He brought her milk to drink, he made her a pillow from a rug, and he hung his cloak over the doorway so that the wind could be kept away.

Their little donkey was with them in the stable too. He ate his supper hungrily, looking round at Mary and Joseph as he munched. Mary smelt the oxen, and felt the warmth their bodies made. She saw their breath steaming in the light of the lantern hung from a nail.

And that night Jesus was born to Mary, in the little stable at Bethlehem. Mary held Him closely in her arms, looking at Him with joy and love. The oxen looked round too, and the little donkey stared with large eyes. The doves watched and cooed softly. The little Son of God was there!

'Joseph, bring me the clothes I had with me,' said Mary. 'I thought perhaps the Baby would be born whilst we travelled, and I brought His swaddling-clothes with me.'

In those far-off days the first clothes a baby wore were called swaddling-clothes. He was wrapped round and round in a long piece of linen cloth. Mary took the linen from Joseph, and wrapped the baby in His swaddling-clothes. Then she wondered where to put Him, for she wanted to sleep.

'He cannot lie on this straw,' said Mary, anxiously. 'Oh, Joseph, we have no cradle for our little baby.'

'See,' said Joseph, 'there is a manger here full of soft hay. It will be a cradle for Him.'

Joseph put the tiny Child into the manger, laying Him down carefully in the soft hay. How small He was! How downy His hair was, and how tiny His fingers were!

Then Mary, tired out, fell asleep on the straw, whilst Joseph kept watch beside her, and the Baby slept peacefully in the manger nearby. The lantern light flickered when the wind stole in, and sometimes the oxen stamped on the floor.

That was the first Christmas, the birthday of the little Christ-child. The little Son of God was born, the great teacher of the world – but only Joseph and Mary knew that at last He had come.

No bells rang out at His birth. The people in the inn slept soundly, not guessing that the Son of God was in a nearby stable. Not one person in the town of Bethlehem knew the great news that night.

But the angels in heaven knew the great happening. They must spread the news. They must come to our world and tell someone.

They had kept watch over the city of Bethlehem that night, and they were filled with joy to know that the little Son of God was born.

Who was awake to hear the angels' news? There was no-one in the town awake that night, but on the hillside outside Bethlehem there were some shepherds, watching their sheep.

Good shepherds always watched their sheep at night, in case wolves came to steal the lambs. They took it in turn to watch, and that night, as usual, there was a company of shepherds together, wrapped in their warm cloaks, keeping guard over their flocks.

They talked quietly together. They had much to talk about that night, for they had watched hundreds of people walking and riding

by their quiet fields, on the way to pay their taxes at Bethlehem. It was seldom that the shepherds saw so many people.

As the shepherds talked, looking round at their quiet sheep, a very strange thing happened. The sky became bright, and a great light appeared in it, and shone all round them. The shepherds were surprised and frightened. What was this brilliant light that shone in the darkness of the night?

They looked up fearfully. Then in the middle of the dazzling light they saw a beautiful angel. He shone too, and he spoke to them in a voice that sounded like mighty music.

'See,' said one shepherd to another in wonder. 'An angel.'

They all fell upon their knees, and some covered their faces with their cloaks, afraid of the dazzling light. They were trembling.

Then the voice of the angel came upon the hillside, full of joy and happiness.

'Fear not; for, behold, I bring you good tidings of great joy, which shall be to all people. For unto you is born this day in the city of David a Saviour, which is Christ the Lord. And this shall be a sign unto you; Ye shall find the Babe wrapped in swaddling clothes, lying in a manger.'

The shepherds listened in the greatest wonder. They were simple country men, and it was hard for them to understand what was happening, and what the angel meant. The Son of God was born in Bethlehem – not far from them? How could that be?

They gazed at the angel in awe, and listened to this wonderful being with his great, over-shadowing wings. As they looked, another strange thing happened, which made the shepherds tremble even more.

The dark sky disappeared, and in its place came a crowd of shining beings, bright as the sun, filling the whole sky. Everywhere the shepherds looked there were angels, singing joyfully.

'Glory to God in the highest,' sang the host of angels, 'and on earth peace, good will towards men. Glory to God in the highest, and on earth peace, good will towards men.'

Over and over again the angels' voices sang these words, and the

shepherds, amazed, afraid and wondering, listened and marvelled. They had never before imagined such a host of shining angels, never before heard on their quiet hillside such a wonderful song. Surely all the angels in heaven were over Bethlehem that night.

Then, as the shepherds watched, the dazzling light slowly faded away, and the darkness of the night came back. The angels vanished with the light, and at last all that could be heard was a faint echo of their voices, still singing 'Glory to God in the highest.'

And then the sky was quite dark again, set with twinkling stars that had been out-shone by the glory of the angels. A sheep bleated and a dog barked. There was nothing to show that heaven had opened to the shepherds that night.

The frightened men were silent for a time, and then they began to talk in low voices that gradually became louder.

'They were angels. How dazzling they were. We saw angels. They came to us, the shepherds on the hillside.'

'It couldn't have been a dream. Nobody could dream like that.'

'I was frightened. I hardly dared to look at the angels at first.

'Why did they come to us? Why should they choose men like us to sing to?'

'You heard what the first angel said – he said a Saviour had been born to us, Christ the Lord. He said that He was born in the City of David tonight – that means in Bethlehem, for Bethlehem is the City of David!'

'Can it be true?'

'Why should all the angels of heaven come and tell us this? Are we the only ones awake in Bethlehem? Oh, what wonderful news this is. I can hear the angels' song in my head still.'

'We will go and find the little King. I want to see Him.'

'We cannot go at midnight. And how do we know where He is?'

'We *must* go! Why should the angels have come to tell us this news, and even told us that the babe is wrapped in swaddling clothes lying in a manger, if they had not meant us to go and worship Him?'

'Why should the Holy Child be put in a manger? Surely He should have a cradle!'

'He must have been born to one of the late travellers, who could find no room at the inn. They must have had to put Him in a manger. I am going to see.'

The shepherds, excited and full of great wonder, went down the hillside to Bethlehem. They left their dogs to guard the sheep, all but one who went with them.

Soon they came to the inn, and, at the back, where the stable was built into the hillside cave, they saw a light. 'Let us go to the stable and see if the Son of God is there,' whispered one shepherd. So, treading softly, they went round to the back of the inn, and came to the entrance of the stable. Across it was stretched Joseph's rough cloak to keep out the wind. The shepherds peered over it into the stable.

They saw what the angel had told them – a babe wrapped in swaddling clothes, lying in a manger!

On the straw, asleep, was Mary. Nearby was Joseph, keeping watch over her and the Child.

'There's the Baby,' whispered the shepherds, in excitement. 'In the manger, wrapped in swaddling clothes. There is the Saviour, the little Son of God.'

Joseph and Mary heard the low voices, and Joseph went to see who was outside the entrance. 'What do you want?' he asked.

Then the shepherds told Joseph about the great light in the sky, and the singing angels. They told him that the first bright angel had said they would find the babe lying in a manger, so they had come to find Him.

Mary heard what they said. She lifted the child from the manger and took Him on her knee. The shepherds knelt down before Him and worshipped Him. Again and again they told the wondering Mary all that had happened. She held her child close, and marvelled at what she heard. Angels had come to proclaim the birth of her tiny Son!

The oxen stared, and the dog pressed close to his master, wondering at the strange happenings of the night. Then, seeing that Mary was looking tired, the shepherds went at last, walking softly in the night.

'We will tell everyone the news tomorrow!' said the shepherds.
'Everyone! What will they say when they know that whilst they slept
we have seen angels?'

'What was the song the angels sang?' said one. 'And what did the
first angel say?'

'He said'Fear not, for behold I bring you good tidings of great
joy,'' said another. 'And the other angels sang'Glory to God in the
highest …'' '

Up the hill they went, back to their sheep, sometimes looking up
into the sky to see if an angel might once again appear. All through

that night they talked eagerly of the angels, the Holy Child in the stable, and of Mary, His gentle mother.

The next day they told everyone of what had happened to them in the night, and many people went to peep in at the stable, to see the little Child.

Mary held Him close to her, and thought often of the angel she herself had seen some months before. She thought of the excited shepherds, and the host of shining angels they too had seen and heard. Her baby was the little Son of God. Mary could hardly believe such a thing was true.

Far far away from Bethlehem in a land that lay to the east, there lived some wise and learned men. At night these men studied the stars in the heavens. They said that the stars showed them the great thoughts of God. They said that when a new star appeared, it was God's way of telling men that some great thing was happening in the world.

Then, one night, a new star appeared in the sky, when the wise men were watching. The second night the star was brighter still. The third night it was so dazzling that its light seemed to put out the twinkling of the other stars.

'God has sent this star to say that something wonderful is happening,' said the wise men. 'We will look in our old, old books, where wisdom is kept, and we will find out what this star means.'

So they studied their old wise books, and they found in them a tale of a great king who was to be born into the world to rule over it. He was to be King of the Jews, and ruler of the world.

'The star seems to stand over Israel, the kingdom of the Jews,' said one wise man. 'This star must mean that the great king is born at last. We will go to worship Him, for our books say He will be the greatest king in the world.'

'We will take him presents of gold and frankincense and myrrh,' said another. 'We will tell our servants to make ready to go with us.'

So, a little while later, when the star was still brilliant every night in the sky, the three wise men set off on their camels. They were like kings in their own country, and a great train of servants followed behind on swift-footed camels. They travelled for many days and nights, and always at night the great star shone before them to guide them on their way.

They came at last to the land of Israel, where the little Jesus had been born. They went of course to the city where the Jewish King lived, thinking that surely the new little King would be there, in the palace at Jerusalem.

Herod was the king there, and he was a wicked man. When his servants came running to tell him that three rich men, seated on magnificent camels, with a train of servants behind them, were at the gates of the palace, Herod bade his servants bring them before him.

The wise men went to see Herod. They looked strange and most magnificent in their turbans and flowing robes. They asked Herod a question that amazed and angered him.

'Where is the child who is born King of the Jews?' they said. 'His

star has gone before us in the east, and we have brought presents for Him, and we wish to worship Him. Where is He?'

"*I* am the King,' said Herod, full of anger. 'What is this child you talk of? And what is this star?'

The wise men told him all they knew. 'We are certain that a great King has been born,' they said, 'and we must find Him. Can you not tell us where He is?'

Herod sat silent for a moment. Who was this new-born King these rich strangers spoke of? Herod did not for a moment disbelieve them. He could see that these men were learned, and knew far more than he did.

'I will find out where this new-born King is, and kill Him,' thought Herod to himself. 'But this I will not tell these men. They shall go to find the Child for me, and tell me where He is – then I will send my soldiers to kill Him.'

So Herod spoke craftily to the wise men. 'I will find out what you want to know. I have wise men in my court who know the sayings of long-ago Jews, who said that in due time a great King would be born. Perhaps this is the Child you mean.'

Then Herod sent for his own wise men and bade them look in the books they had to see what was said of a great king to be born to the Jews. The learned men looked and they found what they wanted to know.

'The King will be born in the city of Bethlehem,' they said.

'Where is that?' asked the wise men.

'Not far away,' said Herod, 'It will not take you long to get there.'

'We will go now,' said the three wise men, and they turned to go.

But Herod stopped them.

'Wait,' he said, 'when you find this new-born King, come back here to tell me where He is, for I too would worship Him.'

The wise men did not know that Herod meant to kill the little King, and not to worship Him. 'You shall be told where He is,' they said. 'We will return here and tell you.'

Then they mounted their camels and went to find the city of Bethlehem, which, as Herod had said, was not far away.

The sun set, and once again the brilliant star flashed into the sky. It seemed to stand exactly over the town of Bethlehem. The strangers, with their train of servants, went down the hill to Bethlehem, their harness jingling, and their jewelled turbans and cloaks flashing in the brilliant light of the great star.

They passed the wondering shepherds, and went into the little city. They stopped to ask a woman to guide them.

'Can you tell us where to find a new-born child?' they asked.

The woman stared at these rich strangers in surprise. She felt sure they must want to know where Jesus was, for everyone knew how angels had come to proclaim His birth.

'Yes', she said, 'you will find the Baby in the Inn yonder. He was born in the stable of the inn, because there was no room for Him. There have been many people already who have come to visit Him. You will find Him there with His mother.'

The star seemed to stand right over the stable to which the woman pointed. The wise men felt sure it was the right one. They made their way to it.

When Mary saw these three magnificent men kneeling before her tiny Baby, she was amazed. Angels had come to proclaim His birth, shepherds had worshipped Him – and now here were three great men kneeling before Him.

'We have found the little King,' said one wise man. 'We have brought Him kingly presents. Here is gold for Him, a gift for a king.'

'And here is sweet-smelling frankincense,' said another.

'And I bring Him myrrh, rare and precious,' said the third. These were indeed kingly gifts, and Mary looked at them in wonder, holding the Baby closely against her. He was her own Child, but He seemed to belong to many others too – to the angels in heaven, to the simple shepherds in the fields, to wise and rich men of far countries. He had been born for the whole world, not only for her.

The wise men left and went to stay for the night at the inn. There was room for them, because the travellers who had thronged the little city had left some time before.

'Tomorrow we will go back to Herod and tell him where the new-born King is, so that he may come and worship Him,' said the wise men. But in the night God sent dreams to them, to warn them not to return to Herod, but to go back to their country another way.

So they mounted their camels, and returned to their country without going near Jerusalem, where Herod lived.

In vain Herod waited for the three wise men to return. His servants soon found out that they had been to Bethlehem but had returned home another way. This made Herod so angry that he hardly knew what he was doing.

First he sent his soldiers after the wise men to stop them, but they were too far away. Then he made up his mind to find the new-born Baby and kill Him.

But no-one knew where the Child was, nor did they even know how old He might be. The wise men themselves had not known how

old the Baby was. Herod sat on his throne, his heart filled with anger.

'Call my soldiers to me,' he said at last.

They came before him, and Herod gave them a cruel and terrible command.

'Go to the village of Bethlehem and kill every boy-child there who is under two years old,' he said. 'Go to the villages round about and kill the young baby-boys there too. Let no one escape.'

The soldiers rode off, their harness jingling loudly. They rode down the hill to Bethlehem, and once again the quiet shepherds stared in wonder at strange visitors. But soon, alas, they heard the screams and cries of the mothers whose little sons had been killed, and they knew that something dreadful was happening.

Every boy-child was killed by the cruel soldiers, and when their terrible work was done, they rode off again, past the watching shepherds, to tell Herod that his commands had been obeyed.

'There is no boy-child under two years old left in Bethlehem or the villages nearby,' said the captain of the soldiers, and Herod was well pleased.

'The new-born King is dead,' he thought. 'I have been clever. I have killed the baby who might one day have been greater than I am.'

But Jesus was not killed. He was safe. On the night that the wise men had left Mary, the little family had gone to bed, and were asleep. But, as Joseph slept, an angel came to him in his dreams, and spoke to him.

'Arise,' said the shining angel. 'Take the young Child and His mother, and flee into Egypt, and stay there until I tell you to return; for Herod will seek the young Child to destroy Him.'

Joseph awoke at once. He sat up. The angel was gone, but the words he had said still sounded in Joseph's ears. Joseph knew that there was danger near, and he awoke Mary at once.

'We must make ready and go,' he said, and he told her what the angel had said. Then Mary knew they must go, and she went to put her few things into a bundle, and to lift up the baby Jesus. Joseph went to get the little donkey, and soon, in the silence of the night, the four of them fled away secretly.

They went as quickly as they could, longing to pass over into the land of Egypt, which did not belong to Herod. He would have no power over them there.

So, when Herod's soldiers came a little later to the city of Bethlehem, Jesus was not there. He was safe in Egypt, where Herod could not reach Him.

And there, until it was safe for Him to return to His own country, the little new-born King lived and grew strong and kind and loving. No-one knew He was a king. His father was a carpenter, and His friends were the boys of the villages around.

But His mother knew. Often she remembered the tale of the shepherds who had seen the angels in the sky, and she remembered too the three wise men who had come to kneel before her baby. She still had the wonderful presents they had given to her for Him. He would one day be the greatest king in the world.

But it was not by power or riches or might that the Baby in the stable grew to be the greatest man the world has ever seen. It was by something greater than all these – by LOVE alone.

That is the story of the first Christmas, which we remember to this day, and which we keep with joy and delight.

A Red Fox Book

Published by Random House Children's Books, 20 Vauxhall Bridge Road, London SW1V 2SA. A division of Random House UK Ltd London Melbourne Sydney Auckland Johannesburg and agencies throughout the world

First published in 1944 by Macmillan & Co Ltd. Red Fox edition 1993. Text © Darrell Waters Ltd 1944. Illustrations © Alan Fraser 1992. All rights reserved.
Enid Blyton's signature mark is a Registered Trade Mark of Darrell Waters Ltd.

Printed in Hong Kong

RANDOM HOUSE UK Limited Reg. No. 954009

ISBN 0-09-938031-5